Cowboy Cougan

Red Cloud Wolverton

Copyright © 2019 by Ivan "Red Cloud" Wolverton

All rights reserved.

No part of this book may be reproduced in any form or by any electronic or mechanical means including information storage and retrieval systems, without permission in writing from the publisher.

This is a work of fiction. Names, characters, businesses, places, events, locales, and incidents are either the products of the author's imagination or used in a fictitious manner. Any resemblance to actual persons, living or dead, or actual events is purely coincidental.

Printed in the United States of America

First Printing March 2019

ISBN 978-1-68454-045-7 Paperback

Published by: Book Services
                www.BookServices.us

Contents

Dedication v

Chapter One 1
Chapter Two 7
Chapter Three 28
Chapter Four 33
Chapter Five 49
Chapter Six 58

Glossary 65

About the Author 68

About the Illustrator 69

Cowboy Cougan

Dedication

To my old-time cowboy friends—

    Sam Mandeville, one hell of a cowboy.

        Correy Kole, for saving my life
            and being the best horseman I've ever known.

Cowboy Cougan

Chapter One

Cougan Banks, looking out across the valley from the back of his little roan horse, wondered why he had taken the job of staying for the winter in this place called Elk Basin, forty miles over the rugged snow-clogged mountains to the nearest settlement. He thought, "What if my horse should fall on me? What if I bust a leg? It'd probably be the middle of next summer before they'd find my old sun-parched bones, and by that time, they wouldn't be no good to me or to anyone else for that matter.

"Right! But what the heck, he thought, as he studied his horse's ears, trying to guess just when old Toy would spook at a little snowshoe rabbit that was digging away at something.

"A feller only lives oncet, and if he's enjoying his life with what he's doing, well then he's pretty well off."

About that time, this "little" horse called Toy, who really wasn't so little, since he weighed close to 1,300 pounds all slimmed down, decided he'd seen about enough of that rabbit's capers he cared to, so he just naturally whirled and bogged his head and made a few jumps, just to see if the tall, slim, fellow they called Cougan was really asleep or if he was just daydreaming. A couple of jumps and Toy was satisfied that Cougan boy was hard to catch asleep, since by the time he'd hit the ground on the first jump, Cougan had already read off the first few lines of "Crockett's Law," [1] taking a little hair as a souvenir.

But someday, Cougan thought, "Old Toy will really put his heart into it, and then I will find the truth of the story that came with Toy when he was cut to his string, twelve years old, having sooner or later bucked off every man that had him in his string.

"We'll worry about that when the time comes," Cougan mused, as he herded his thinking back to why he had asked for this winter camp.

"Twenty-five years old—no sweetheart, no relatives, and not a blamed thing but my outfit and the few lousy wages I got coming.

"Let's see," he went on, as he mentally counted the wages up on his fingers; October—yeah, he'd been to town in October and gotten rid of his September check, But he hadn't drawn any of October's, so there'd be that and November, and here it was almost Christmas. That would be right at four hundred fifty bucks. And if he stayed here in Elk Basin until the first of April? Hmm! He half echoed out loud as he tried to visualize the staggering sum of nine hundred dollars. All his own and all saved up in one bunch!

---

[1] See the Glossary for Cowboy Terms.

Chapter One

"Wow!" He uttered as he shook his head. "With a stake like that to dream of, it seems plenty worthwhile to spend these six months in this godforsaken beautiful little valley. Who knows? Maybe I can put it to good use, and make something of my worthless self, besides just a drifting cowboy."

He poked on along, thinking of a jillion different things like how riding a tired horse was just like pumping a bicycle up hill." Not that Toy was really tired, but probably just contrary because he wanted to go back to camp.

As usually happens when a fellow's trying to think of other things, so as to shut something out of his mind, it keeps popping up.

Cougan's thoughts finally drifted back to Christmas. Christmas celebrations! Boy, he'd had some good ones! One in particular, he liked was in '44, when he had been repping over in the islands for his rich Uncle Sammy. He'd been put out on one of them scouting parties Christmas morning, but nothing exciting had happened. He guessed the enemy had all either been killed or had pulled out somehow.

Anyway, he decided that this Christmas wouldn't really be so bad after all as he remembered the bottle of Old Grandad he'd stashed away special for the occasion. It probably wouldn't be quite as wild a time as Christmas '44, but by gosh, he'd have a little companionship after all.

With these brighter thoughts in his mind, he gently touched old Toy up a bit and skimmed out across the snow-skiffed meadow, without a worry in the world. Out onto a low ridge they loped before pulling up for a breather.

"Well, Toy, you old dirty son-of-a-gun, what does it feel like to have someone on you who isn't afraid to move you out?"

Triumphantly, Cougan grinned as he tried to smooth Toy's mane out.

"You'll be a gentle nag come spring, feller, unless I'm done in."

Cougan then pulled the makins out and slowly twisted himself a quirley as he sat studying the sky.

"What a prize gunsel I am," he thought, as he studied the dark, heavy storm clouds that were building up behind him. "Here I've been daydreaming along in the sunshine and have gotten a good many miles away from camp, and now that looks like one heck of a blizzard building up. Toy, old son, I s'pose we better be turning our tails and see if we can't make it home before them snowballs go to hitting us."

The dark storm clouds were building up fast then; as only they can do in rough mountainous country. Thirty minutes from the time Cougan had started back toward camp, the sky had closed in, like putting a lid on a kettle.

"By golly, Toy, if we don't get lost in a blizzard before we get home, I reckon we'll be lucky," Cougan said half out loud, as the big snowflakes started floating down. "It shore looks like winter has settled on us to stay. Doggone it feller, this country is the jinx. Here we've moped away from camp all day looking for stray cows, when we know we already done got them all; now we've got caught in a storm, with you all tired and me hungry enough to tackle a good sized bear, just to chew on him a while. It wouldn't be so bad now if we could go right down across the meadows

Chapter One

to camp. It'd only be, oh, probably five or so many miles, but man, there's so many holes and bogs that way; I'd hate to tackle it on a clear warm summer day, much less in a blizzard.

"Bow your neck and head into it, feller, we might as well face it; there's "No rest for the wicked!" and I reckon that ole boy up there's gonna hand us both some of our back wages for our sins. Come on now, keep a-jogging; it's only about ten miles farther, and we'll be home in a couple hours or so."

They had gone on for perhaps a mile and were trying to follow a trail through a wooded hillside that jutted out into the meadow, when Cougan pulled Toy up of a sudden to listen. He swore he heard the low rumble of an airplane. Preposterous! It must have been his ears playing tricks on him. What would a plane be doing in this rough country? Why, one seldom flew over, even in the summer time.

He started to move Toy on, but pulled him up with a start as he strained to see through the snow-filled sky. "By gawd!" he exclaimed. He had heard a plane. He knew it, as he switched his head from side to side again, trying to pierce that snow-blanketed sky.

"Dammit, Toy, that feller better pull up or he's gonna light right in our lap!" broke from Cougan's mouth, as he saw the huge plane plowing through the tree tops, heading straight toward him.

The cold steel of the spurs was driven into Toy's quivering sides, unmercifully, for there was only a split second's time to grasp the chance in a thousand of being able to get clear. For once in his life, Toy tried to run when jabbed with the spurs instead of going to pitching. Two terrific jumps, Cougan later remembered Toy making and then the deafening roar and explosion. Man and horse were knocked flat!

Cougan landed clear of Toy's tumbling body. When the world quit spinning, and he struggled back to his feet, he found that he still had ahold of one bridle rein.

Toy lunged to his feet and tried to break loose, but Cougan, an old hand with horses, knew that Toy might be pretty valuable presently and managed to hang onto him, finally quieting him down enough to be tied to a tree with his lass rope. Then he broke for the wreckage of the devastated plane, thinking that at any minute it might burst into flames. If there were any survivors, he'd have to move pronto.

Chapter Two

The main body of the wreckage had finally come to a stop about a hundred yards past where Cougan had narrowly made his escape. There had been one explosion when it hit, the blast being what had knocked him and his horse, galley-west.

As Cougan plowed his way through the tangle of broken jack pines, he could see flames licking at some part of the plane. He figured it was part of a motor, but it was hard to see anything clearly with the snow still coming down so gentle and peaceful, as though nothing had happened.

Cougan was so busy trying to pierce the blanket of snow as he ran forward, looking for any chance survivors, that he didn't have much time to pick his footing. The first thing he knew, he was falling, trying to scramble back to his feet, to keep running, with the event that he finally took a headlong dive into the snow-covered ground. Mighty lucky he was, for he hadn't even had time to complete his fall, when a second explosion shook the pine trees all around.

As Cougan lay there, hugging the snow-covered ground and listening to the debris as it whistled through the air, he wondered if Toy would break loose and leave him afoot with a bunch of half-dead survivors here for him to look after.

In an instant, the world was peaceful again. The second explosion must have snuffed out the fire completely. Lunging to his feet, Cougan's hopes for any survivors plummeted. The big plane had been completely blown into unrecognizable fragments.

He walked out slowly through the wreckage-strewn hillside. Although he had lost hope, he still felt the urge to prowl through the litter. There might be something, some clue, or—he didn't know what, but there might be something that would soon be covered with snow. There wasn't much that was recognizable, just some clothing and pieces of luggage.

Cougan had to stop and build himself a smoke. What he'd seen in the war hadn't bothered him near like what this did. He tore his first paper in two with trembling fingers, and as he fished the second one from the book, he said aloud to himself, "Now settle down feller, and take it easy here; there's something that's gotta be done, and you're the only one capable." After a couple of chestfuls of smoke, he finally got his stomach to stay settled and proceeded with the gruesome task.

There must have been several people aboard the plane, he thought, as he commenced to bring the remains to the center of the area and lay them together. It was a sickening undertaking, but it had to be done. He couldn't just leave them scattered around in the snow.

Chapter Two

Finally, he decided there wasn't much more he could do at present, so he covered up the human forms with what he could find and then headed to where he'd left old Toy. "Cripes," he thought, "I'd sooner be laid under myself than to have to go through that again!"

As Cougan stumbled along back to where he'd left his horse, he thought of what he'd have to do now. He'd have to get out to civilization and notify somebody about the wreckage. "That is, if it ever quits snowing so's I can find my way out of these mountains," he mused. He had covered about half the distance back to his horse when he was stalled in his tracks. He thought he heard something like a person's moan off to the left.

It must have been the wind," he figured, as he stood observing the fast-fading light of day. "She's started to whoop up in the last half hour or so, and it'll probably really be howling by the time I reach camp,"

The sound came again, as he was starting to move on. This time he knew for sure, it was made by a human.

"But that's incredible," he thought, as he remembered the way that the plane had been blown to bits. Nevertheless, he came to where a human form was sprawled on the ground in less time than it takes to imagine it. At first glance, he could see that whoever it was, was in bad shape. One leg, he couldn't tell at first which one, was at an odd angle to the body, which could mean only one thing—It was sure busted up. As he bent over the figure for further examination, the semi-darkness of the fast-fading day revealed the long, dark, wavy hair of a beautiful lady.

"My gawd!" he murmured, as he observed the deep gash along the side of her head. "If you pull through this, you can thank your guardian angel."

With further examination, Cougan decided she still had a fairly strong pulse, and she didn't seem to be breathing too hard. The next thing he guessed he'd better try to do was to see if he could straighten out that broken leg. It seemed to be a fairly straight break, about halfway between the hip and the knee. The girl had on slacks, which made it rather inconvenient to tell if the bone had broken the skin or not; however, since there wasn't any blood, Cougan decided it must not have. When he pulled the leg around straight, the lady moaned, but didn't come to, for which he was thankful, as he knew it was hurting her enough with her being unconscious.

The bone seemed to be pretty much in line, as near as he could feel. The thing now was to keep it there. He studied his options as he started unbuckling his chaps.

"Them old batwing chaps!" he thought. Man, he'd used them for everything, from beating out a prairie grass fire to using them for an umbrella oncet for a lady caught in a rain.

He found it rather a problem to hold her leg steady and wind the chaps around it, but he finally got it done.

"The two legs of the chaps wound around her leg makes a fair splint," he decided, as he fished through his Levi's pocket looking for some leather lacing he'd put there the other day.

While he worked, a plan had been running through his mind as to how he'd get her back to his camp. To pack

Chapter Two

her on Toy was out of the question. He had an old team of broncs back at camp, but with the storm looking like it was bound to develop into a monster blizzard, he doubted if he could get home and back to this spot in time to be of any help to this girl. He had to get her inside and out of this weather pronto. He'd have to make some sort of a sled and strap her to it, so's he could drag her home with old Toy.

Tying the lacing to hold the chaps-splint in place, he straightened up, pulled his jacket off, and spread it over her, as he peered out through the darkness trying to locate something he could use for a sled.

There appeared to be a small clearing a short way left of where she was lying, and he decided he'd better carry her over there and build up a bonfire before he rigged up a sled. With the darkness and this here snow blowing in at a slant, he was afraid he might lose her here in the timber.

It wasn't any easy task to pick her unconscious form up and hold that broken leg straight. After a couple of attempts, he ripped the lining from his coat and tore it into long strips, using these to bind the broken leg to the good one. It was still quite a problem, carrying her through the tangled, fallen jack pines; he most near slipped down a couple times, but finally he made it out, laying her down by some brush where the snow hadn't melted any, and the pine needles underneath were dry enough that he didn't have much trouble getting a good fire going.

A piece of tin off that plane would make a good sled, if it hadn't all gotten snowed under, he figured, as he set out in search. He hadn't gone very far back toward the wreckage when he slipped on something, almost going down. It was hard to see much here in the dark, but that sure felt like what he was looking for. There under the snow, when he bent over a little closer to the ground, he could see the end of what he'd slipped on, sticking up out of the snow.

No, he didn't grin with delight when he pulled the object from the snow and found it to be just what he had in mind. For there was another thought trying to worm its way to the top now: What would old Toy think of this contraption? True, he had dragged a good many imaginary calves to the branding fire on him without much trouble, but roping weeds and bushes would probably be a long ways from resembling a little bawling calf.

With a shrug of his shoulders, he started back toward the fire in the opening, thinking that the excitement might not be near finished on this old hill tonight. By the time Cougan had gotten back to the opening and built the fire up, he'd decided the night was gonna be a bad one. The snow was still falling, and that old wind seemed to be pretty ferocious. As he hunkered his back side up to the fire, he studied the sheet of metal he'd found. "Must be close to eight feet long and better'n three wide. Reckon I can leave that end curled up like it is and sort of pound the sides up; I can fill the bottom with pine boughs. That ought to make a fair bed. Reckon I can punch some holes in the end and sides to pull it by, and tie her on it," he mused, as he felt his six-shooter under his left arm.

Now maybe you think it sounds strange—Cougan, a full-grown man, packing a six-shooter here in the last part of the year 1950 A.D., but for you people who scoff: when you're forty miles from the nearest civilization, and you haven't got anything to ride but a bunch of owl-headed old ponies that think a man is something they're supposed to get into a jackpot and then fall over on him or buck him off and set him afoot—well, for you fellers who know not that these conditions still exist, for your information, a

Chapter Two

six-shooter is one handy piece of equipment to have along when you're riding all alone out in the mountain-desert country.

"What's this?" you say, what good would the so-called six-gun be to him if his horse bucked him off and ran away?"

Well, sure; you got a point there. All he'd need would be a good pair of legs and lots of wind. He could invent his own cuss words as he hoofed it along. Where that old six-gun would really come in handy, though, would be if that old cayuse stepped in a hole and broke a leg, or if he slipped and fell and lit on top of that poor feller, which often enough happens in the winter on the frozen, slick ground. Yeah, usually a horse can scamper right back to his feet, but just suppose that he couldn't get up, and you were lying with a leg under him. Of course you could cut his throat with your pocketknife, if you could reach it, but just look how much easier it'd be with a six-gun, after you blowed the top of his head off. Then you could proceed to cut your riggin' away and whittle yourself loose. Why would he use a shoulder holster to pack it in? Well, he ain't gonna be doing any fast drawing, so it's just more logical to pack it where it's out of the way and in the dry in case of a storm.

Anyhow, Cougan packed a six-shooter, .38 caliber, Smith & Wesson Police Special revolver to be exact, and he swore he didn't care what anybody thought, as long as he was by himself in a country as big as this, he'd have that six-gun with him. The reports as he fired the holes through the front and sides of the sled sounded awfully loud and disturbing here on the snowy hillside. One puncture through the upcurled front end and four on the sides, using six cartridges. He'd used four of the cartridges he carried in loops in the strap he wore that ran from the shoulder holster up around his neck.

"Two cartridges left," he thought, as he punched the last hole. "Well, that's probably more'n I'll shoot all the rest of the winter."

After he'd gathered more pine boughs for the bed, he built the fire up again. After checking to see that the girl seemed okay, he struck out to get Toy, if he was still there.

He had a little trouble locating the spot as there wasn't much to go by. It was too dark and still snowing too hard to see very far. "This is sorta like hunting for a penny in the desert. Trying to locate a light-colored horse on a snow-filled night," he thought, except this isn't quite so warm." He hunted quite a while and then almost bumped into Toy, just as he had about decided that maybe he had jerked loose. Toy wasn't much too pleased about being mounted and headed up the hill the wrong way from camp, but Cougan finally persuaded him which way he should go. He wasn't very hard to get close to the fire, although he didn't like it. Like most cowhorses, he'd seen a good many such fires on cold, frosty mornings and long rainy days.

Cougan wasn't of a superstitious nature, but he had most always yielded to the impulses of premonitions and intuition with good results, so he made a few quick decisions, as he stood prodding the fire. The first thing would be to heap up the logs to make a roaring fire, for it was hard to tell where we'll be when Toy gets over his fit, he soberly reflected, as he set about the task. Next, he guessed he'd better take off his six-shooter, and leave it by the girl. Its weight would sure be a hindrance with old Toy breaking in two, the way he knew he would. Besides, if he and Toy got out in the brush all tangled up, and she came to, before

Chapter Two

he could get back to her, maybe she wouldn't get quite so scared. Not that she looked like the type to get easily frightened. Come to think about it, he really hadn't gotten a good look at her yet. It was too dark to tell much, except she did have dark hair!

After he had placed his six-gun by her side, he felt for her wrist to check on her pulse. He noticed that her left hand was some skinned up and felt like it was starting to swell a bit, but she didn't have any ring on it. Her pulse seemed to be pretty strong, and she seemed to be breathing fairly well.

He had brought his saddle slicker over and spread it over her in place of the remains of his old Levi jumper. She had a pretty heavy coat on, and with the old slicker to break the cool air, maybe she would be warm enough. He figured there wasn't much more he could do for her, till he got her back to his camp, but what then? He didn't know. As he straightened up to go back to Toy, he thought about his chaps wrapped around her legs. He'd sure like to have them to make this ride with, but she needed them more than he did.

He tore the remains of the jumper into strips as he walked over to the sled. Part of the strips were used to make loops at the front to tie the lass tow rope on, and he ran the rest through the holes in the sides, bringing them back and tying the ends together in the middle. When he got ready to haul her home, he would tie these over the top of her, to make sure he didn't lose her out of the sled. He'd thrown his lass rope down on the sled when he rode up, so now he unthreaded the hondo, ran the end of the rope through the loops made from the jumper strips, and then rethreaded the hondo, so he didn't have to tie a knot in his lariat.

As he stood doing this, he wondered why he hadn't just tied the Levi strips through the loop in the first place. "Guess I was just concentrating too much on how that old Toy son-of-a-gun is going to perform here directly."

Toy was close enough that Cougan didn't have to move the sled any for the rope to reach, so he just let the coils feed out, as he walked slowly toward Toy, humming the tune to some soft song, like "Kokomo Island," trying to keep Toy from noticing he was a little nervous; that's what he was doing.

Toy stood ankle-deep in snow now, with his head sort of hanging half down. His ears were tipped back slightly, and his eyes seemed to be sparkling with the devil that was there just waiting. Cougan pulled his cinch up tight and turned Toy, facing the sled and rope. As he stood a moment brushing the snow from his saddle, he thought, "Ol' Lady Luck, if you ever been on my side, I hope you're here tonight! Oh well, what the Hell! We'll know soon." He shrugged his shoulders as he gathered up the slack from his reins with his left hand and sought out the horn with his right.

Toy was one horse that had to be watched when he was mounted. Since it's the easiest way to tell what a horse is going to do by watching his eye when mounting, that's what Cougan did to get an even start. He was not more than halfway to the saddle when Toy dropped his head and tried to whirl away; however, with the short grip Cougan had on the near rein, in one short instant, he was able to check his movement and whirl Toy to the left, bringing him back under himself, thus making a clean job of mounting. But now all hell broke loose!

Chapter Two

When Toy had whirled, it had jerked the rope and the sled lacing off the toboggan, and being empty, it had come slipping right across the snow. Cougan turned the rope loose as soon as he saw he couldn't pull Toy up.

The first few jumps weren't bad, high and crooked, but the snow seemed to be slowing Toy up a bit. The first three or four jumps put Toy across the clearing. Cougan, knowing he had no control over Toy with the bridle, knew there was only one thing left to do if he didn't want to go bucking out into the timber, and that was to spur him high and hard in the shoulder on one side. That would usually turn him; so that's just what he did, and he got results.

When Cougan hit him in the shoulder, old Toy sucked 'er back so hard and fast, he was almost unseated. That little jab of shoulder spurring was all Toy was looking for. He had quit fooling. He was swapping ends now with most every jump, first suckin' 'er back one way and then another, coming down on one low shoulder, and then the other; but still that monster of a cowboy clung up there, driving the cold steel of those spurs way deep into the shoulder muscles with every jump.

Cougan could feel himself getting weak; every muscle in his body seemed to be paralyzed. "Gawd, I'd like to get off this damn, howling, jerking, loco son-of-Satan! Gawd damn ye! Buck, if that's what ye want!" He cursed, as he drove his spurs home and exercised a vocabulary that could have embarrassed most any decent mule skinner.

As he sat up there spurring and swearing, he could feel the warm blood spraying out, running down the corners of his mouth, but still old Toy kept jerking into the air and suckin' 'er back, hitting the ground so stiff-legged, it would most near drive Cougan through him. Still, he clung up there, clawing and spurring and cursing Toy for everything he'd ever done from the day of his birth on.

Several minutes went by. Cougan wasn't sure where they were, but he thought they were still in the clearing. Still old Toy was mopping 'er up. But now, he was so weak; he'd just got his spurs into Toy's belly and was just hanging on with 'em by what few cuss words he had left, most of 'em near all used up now. Then he felt Toy slacken, make one big long jump, gallop a few paces, and finally come to a stop.

Cougan sat there for a long time so dazed and exhausted, with his body going through such convulsions, that it was hard to realize old Toy was standing still. There was something awfully bright right in front of him. He was thinking, "It looks like a bonfire, but what the hell would somebody be doing having a wiener roast out here on such a bad night?"

His thoughts raced on helter skelter before his mind cleared enough for him to realize that Toy had stopped right in front of the fire. He sat a minute longer, rubbing his eyes before he dismounted. Toy was standing spraddle-legged, with his head almost touching the ground and his ears both flipped out to the sides, like he didn't even have the strength to hold them up.

Cougan was so weak he had to hang onto the saddle horn as he stood talking to Toy, gently patting his muscles. A stranger, listening, would never have thought there had just been a battle between these two. The way Cougan was whispering sweet nothings to old Toy, he would have sworn it sounded more like the soft, passionate tone of a loving mother soothing her frightened child in the middle of the night.

Chapter Two

For perhaps an hour, he stood there, talking to Toy, and rubbing the quivering muscles. It mattered not what he said, how he told how sorry he was that all this had to happen, and such, for it isn't what is said that counts; it's what comes from the tone of voice that animals learn their trust, or love, or fear. Some way along the line, Cougan had gotten across the median between man and beast, that he didn't just want to be Toy's conqueror, that he also wanted to be friends.

Anyhow, he had about given up on making friends with Toy, who had not moved from the position he took when he stopped; and he had decided to go stir up the fire to warm up a mite. He turned and started to leave. He hadn't taken but a couple steps when he was stopped by a soft nicker. Turning around, he found Toy with his head raised up slightly and ears cocked forward toward him. His eyes even seemed to have a sparkle again, only a friendly one now, Cougan thought, as he walked back and spoke softly, telling Toy, "Come on up to the fire with me."

The first time Cougan had started toward the fire, he had left him ground-reined. He figured Toy was so completely whipped that he wouldn't try to run off. Now he seemed to be coming to life, but not with that mean, grudging outlook on life, that he'd had before.

Toy watched every move Cougan made stirring up the fire. When he had the fire roaring again and had gotten partly warmed up, he decided to pull the sled up to Toy to see what would happen. He started to tie Toy's reins around a piece of log lying by the fire, but Toy seemed so trusting that he ground-reined him again. The sled wasn't very far from the fire, so Cougan dug his lass rope, the lead rope, from the snow, and walked with the end of it back up to Toy. He stood talking a minute, showing Toy the rope.

Once, Toy reached his nose out and sniffed the rope, as if to tell Cougan that everything was all right; he wasn't scared anymore. He gathered up Toy's reins as a precaution and then started pulling the sled toward them hand over hand. Toy sort of half whirled toward the sled and snorted when he first saw it move, but after a soft word and a stroke on the neck from Cougan, he just stood quietly alert with ears cocked forward as the sled was pulled closer.

When Cougan had pulled sled right up close, he reached down and picked up the end of it. Toy snorted again, but then stuck his nose out and smelled the odd-looking contraption. After a minute, he took a step forward and smelled the outfit all over; then he looked up toward Cougan and stuck his nose way out and wrinkled up his upper lip, letting his teeth show, the way horses do, when they smell or taste something new and strange to them. After all of this performance was over, Toy turned partly toward Cougan and sort of shook his head as if to say that everything was okay.

The snow had been falling intermittently ever since the storm had started. Cougan, with no coat or chaps, was half wet and cold clear through. Every time he got away from the fire, he would almost freeze. Finally, after he had placed the pine boughs in the sled, loaded the girl, and secured the bindings, he decided to use his saddle blanket as a windbreaker. He had one big, heavy double-fold Navajo blanket and a sweat pad. He could put the sweat pad over the front and cut a slit crossways in the center of the Navajo to put his head through, like a poncho. Since the blanket was about 30 by 60 inches, that would leave about half in front and the other half across his back. He pulled his piggin' string up tight around his middle, on the outside of the blankets, and this closed up the gapping side fairly good.

Chapter Two

As he gathered up his lass rope and turned toward Toy, he thought, "Well, old feller, we got the girl this time, and it'll probably really be blowing 'er up when we get out of the timber, so why don't you see if you can be as good a horse for the rest of the night as you have been bad so far?"

He turned Toy toward the sled, pulled the lass rope up over his neck, brushed the snow from his saddle, gathered the slack from his reins, and eased aboard. This time, Toy was quite the different horse from what he had been a couple hours previous. However, Cougan was still cautious.

He took a dally with the rope and backed Toy up a step. The sled came forward a little, and Toy didn't seem to mind, so he backed him a couple more steps. Toy took it all in good stride, so now he turned him and made a short circle around the clearing, turning the sled.

Cougan rode back up to the fire, chuckling at his own humor, as he nudged Toy on the neck with his rein hand, and asked him," Do you think I should put the fire out, so it won't burn down the forest out here on this snowy mountainside?"

He was only trying to build up his own courage before he rode out into the night; for he knew himself, that if there was a blizzard raging out in the valley, like he had reason to believe there might be, he would be plumb lucky to reach camp. He knew that if it wasn't for the girl, he would stay right here tonight, but he felt he just had to get her in out of the storm.

"Well, let's go old man," he said to Toy, as he begrudgingly pulled away from the fire and headed down the hill toward the trail he had been forced to leave earlier that evening. "I shore hope we make it home in time to save this poor girl."

As Cougan rode down the hillside, dodging among the trees and trying to pick up the trail, he wondered about the girl. First of all, he worried about her being unconscious all this time. And then he wondered how she had escaped from that flaming wreckage.

A chill wriggled its way up every bone, as he remembered the mess he had left behind. He knew he would have to guide a party back to this place. He almost rode across what he took for the trail, which would have been plumb easy for most people to do in broad daylight, the way everything was getting snowed under. Toy responded to the nudge of the rein across his neck, but with protest. The direction they were traveling would have lined out pretty well across the meadow and on to camp, probably five miles straight across. But the trail turned at almost a right angle away from that straight line, and Toy knew it very well. But outlaw that Toy had been all his life, he had still acquired a fair shot of a good education from the different bronc riders that had him in their string, and he knew better than to disobey reining. Still, though, he tried occasionally taking off the way he wanted to go; only to be immediately informed by rein and spur to follow his rider's direction.

The sled really pulled easy, most near too easy in places, for it would run up on Toy on the steep downhill slopes of washes and such. When this happened, Cougan would either trot up to keep ahead, or if the slope was too long and he worried it might get going too fast and flip over—well, then he would step Toy aside and let the sled stop out ahead, so that he could hold it back.

Chapter Two

As long as he didn't let it get going too fast, it wasn't very hard to keep the sled sliding in a straight line, even though the rope was fastened to the front end. The first time the sled ran up on him, and he had to step aside and let it pass, Cougan thought for a minute that Toy was going to have another one of his conniptions, for he really did get nervous when that outfit came slipping past. He sat and talked to him for all he was worth to make him behave. Even then, he knew he would have gone for a bronc ride, if he hadn't turned Toy crossways off to the side of the trail, so he could see the sled coming, instead of suddenly having it pass him by.

The wind was stepping it up something ferocious when Cougan got out in the open where he had to cross the mouth of a wide side draw. The way this damn wind's blowing," he thought," we'll shore be lucky if we don't completely lose where the trail is supposed to be."

He couldn't keep from worrying about the girl all the while, wondering if she was warm enough. Once he stopped and got off to check the feel of her cheek, and finding that her pulse was getting a little weaker, he decided he could do without the saddle pad that he had under his makeshift poncho.

After placing the pad under the slicker to give her a little more protection, he straightened up and worked his arms vigorously out to the sides and back against his chest, trying to create some heat energy.

The weather had been almost unbearable before he removed the pad. The storm had been blowing head on. As wet as his whole body was after the battle with Toy— well, the cold just seemed to go right through him.

"It's shore tough on us fellers who have been used to good wind-breaking clothes and leather chaps to have to do without them, and on such a night as this," he kidded himself. "But don't be a baby, Cougan, you're lots bigger than she is!"

After a few minutes exercising, he decided the blood was flowing again, and he crawled back on old Toy and trudged on. When he eased back in the saddle this time, he noticed that his legs felt pretty sore, like as if maybe the hide had been peeled off the inside length of both of them.

"Funny," he thought, "I hadn't noticed it before," but after a minute's deliberation, he thought, "It must have been because I was too excited."

He knew the country was level for quite a ways now, so he dallied his rope and stuck the loose end under his leg to secure the dallies, and maybe it would be easier to keep his hands warm. He struggled on for what seemed like years. His teeth rattled so loudly that he could hardly keep his head still. His legs felt like they were frozen where the snow had stuck to his Levi's. All he could feel of his feet was the weight of his spurs. He was sure his toes had fallen off. He had been changing hands, holding the reins with one hand and sitting on the other, but even then, they were both so stiff that he could hardly open his fist to make the switch from hand to hand.

He had been trying to keep the gaps in the sides of his poncho closed with his upper arms, but he was sure the snow was blowing in one side and out the other. All this while, he had been riding solely by instinct, because the trail had been obliterated by the blown snow, almost ever since he had been out in the open. He had been trying to go straight across the opening so he could reach the shelter

Chapter Two

of the timber and circle in the rest of the way to his camp; but now he decided he had turned too far in line. He knew he had ridden much farther since leaving the other side of the draw, than what the distance across it would be.

It was almost impossible now for him to keep any set course of direction. For a while he had travelled according to the angle of the blowing wind, but now it was coming from every which way. A real howling, raging blizzard was taking place in this old basin!

Now here he was, right in the middle of it, not knowing for sure from which direction he'd come and completely perplexed as to what direction to keep going. He knew he had to keep moving. As cold as he was, if he stopped now, he would soon be beyond the stage of reality, perhaps delusional. Already he was beginning to feel warm because his body was so frozen; he knew that was a danger sign, but he couldn't give up now, for he knew that girl back there on the sled was banking on him to get her to safety.

"That girl—" he thought, "I never have gotten a good look at her face, but somehow she seems to arouse memories deep within me.

"Miss, just because I'm freezing ain't cause for me to think like that," he murmured out loud, as he slapped his leg, trying to break the spell he was drifting into.

Toy had resigned himself to Cougan's will, sometime back, and he quit looking off from the direction they were traveling. Now, as though sensing something of the despair Cougan was in, as to what direction to travel, he stopped. Cougan started to nudge him on, but then hesitated, for Toy had his head up and ears cocked way forward, as though he was studying with deep intensity. Presently, he swung his head about a quarter of the way to the right and sort of worked his nose up and down, like he was trying to tell Cougan that this was the direction they should be going.

Cougan was so cold and so turned around that he hardly knew which way was up, so why should he argue with one of God's own outdoor creatures about which way was home he reasoned, as he nudged Toy on with a free rein. Then he tied a knot in his reins and hung them over the dallied rope on the horn. He set about trying to keep what little spark of life was still burning, the tiny spark that he had left.

He had thought about getting off and walking to try to warm up some, but he knew he would surely lose all sense of direction. He guessed he'd best stay mounted and try to keep from thinking of the biting cold now that Toy was picking the course.

He had been working his arms, trying to maintain a little circulation and had about decided he was gaining some, for that warm feeling of freezing to death that he'd had a short while before, had left. In its place, there was just plain biting cold. He had redone his bandanna quite a ways back, taking one wrap around his neck, and after crossing the ends under his chin, pulled them up over his ears and made the knot on the top of his head. His hat kept the makeshift ear muffs in place. As he thought about it, he decided that his ears, unless they were already frozen off, were the only parts of his body that didn't hurt from the cold.

He would have liked to pull his head back through the hole in his poncho, "like a turtle does," he thought. He almost managed a grin, but he knew he had to keep a sharp lookout for anything he might recognize. A bush or weed,

Chapter Two

or anything might be enough to regain his bearings, or at least, to confirm Toy's.

It was really hard to see very far. Occasionally the snow would be whirled so hard that he couldn't even see Toy's ears, but then, at times, he could see several yards through this howling night.

Chapter Three

Cougan worried some about Toy's picking the way. If they were traveling in the direction he surmised they were, well then, they were heading right straight across the valley, right through the rotten pothole-in-the-ground country. Crossing this stretch at night was enough to make a man wonder, for the last time he had been down in this area, he'd had the ground cave out from under him. His horse had only broken through up to his belly, and had lunged back to solid ground as he bailed off him.

"But that was in broad daylight," he frowned. "If we hit something like that tonight, we'll be in a hell of a fix."

Toy had been travelling with his nose almost touching the ground for quite a ways. "He must be worried about this damn rotten plummy-bed country too," Cougan thought, as he strained his eyes, trying to pierce the blanket of whirling snow.

Presently Toy stopped after emitting a snort, which sounded as though he was pretty skeptical about some-

Chapter Three

thing. The snow was blowing so hard that Cougan couldn't see the ground, but he knew Toy wouldn't have stopped unless there was something wrong; he picked up the reins and sat shivering, waiting for the snowy air to clear up a bit.

After another minute, he could see the ground, or rather, he could see a large black area ahead of them, where the ground should have been. After sitting and studying the hole for some time, he decided he recognized the spot. He had seen three or four big cave-ins like this down here, not very deep, just four or five feet, but even that would mess things up somewhat, he thought.

He hadn't paid close attention to any of these potholes. He had just checked to see that there weren't any cattle down in any of them. There had been one hole that was longer and narrower than the others, and it seemed like it had been almost out to the solid country in the left end of the rotten part. He guessed he would have to chance it that way, as he reined Toy to the left and started on. He could only go a few paces, and then he would have to stop and wait for the snow to clear up so he could see again.

"We're not getting anywhere like this," he thought, as he had to stop Toy again so he could pull the loose end of his rope from under his cold, stiff leg, take a half hitch on the horn, and then step off into the snow. This seemed like the safest way to get back to solid ground he figured, as he tried to get his cold, frozen knees to bend a little. He took a couple steps in front of Toy, and then had to stop to keep from falling in a heap. His legs were so numb they didn't seem to have any feeling from the hips on down. After a few minutes of rubbing and working them, he got the muscles to liven up enough to pack himself clumsily in a forward direction.

Cougan led Toy until he couldn't walk any more. His body felt better, but each step was becoming an effort, and he knew that he was still at least two miles from camp. That big hole had been the one he thought it was, and he had hit solid ground shortly after circling the end of it. He kept walking for a ways, so maybe he could warm up a bit more. As he walked back by Toy's shoulder, he pulled the reins up around his neck, and told him, "I'm all fagged out this time, old feller, so see if you can stand still for me now."

Toy had his head cocked a little to the left, like he was watching, but he never offered to move a muscle until Cougan had remounted, reached down, and patted him on the neck, saying, "Let's go home now, old man." In a minute Toy was leading the way again. It seemed to Toy's way of thinking that Cougan had gotten a little off course in his walking.

A half hour later they came to a fence. "My horse-trap fence!" Cougan beamed, as he made out the wire after Toy had stopped. There was a gate on his side of the meadow, he knew, as he sat wondering which way down the fence it would be. Lost as he was and getting ready to turn Toy to the left, Toy started on his own account and turned to the right. They didn't travel more than a couple hundred feet before they came to it.

"By golly, you're the smarter of us two," Cougan said, as he switched his reins to his right hand and reached out with his left to pull the wire loop over the top of the gate stick so he wouldn't have to dismount. He went about the gate opening cautiously, for the last time he had tried to open a wire gate without getting off Toy, he'd gone for a bronc ride. Toy just wouldn't stand for his reaching out to that side that way a'tall. Now he stood with ears alert and

Chapter Three

head slightly turned, watching what was going on, but he didn't offer to make a move.

"I'll come back and shut this some warm day," Cougan said out loud, as he pulled the gate from the bottom wire loop, and then threw the outfit as far out of the way as possible. He had to sort of turn Toy out a ways, so as to pull the sled up to where it would clear the gate post, before he turned in and headed for the last leg of his journey.

Cougan's spirits were much higher now that he was in his own horse pasture. He felt so good that he tried to whistle a tune, but his jaws and cheeks were so cold and stiff that he couldn't pucker up, so he just grinned inwardly and thought of how nice it would be to get back to his camp and build a fire in the fireplace. He'd put old Toy in the shed of a barn and feed him. Then he'd cook himself a big pot of coffee. "Dad gum," he thought, as his stomach growled, "Seems like it's been a month since I last ate." But then he forgot about his stomach as he thought about the girl on the sled and all that he would have to do, wondering if she would pull through.

When he got to the cabin, he pulled the sled up as close as he could get it. He got off Toy and dragged the sled onto the porch, thinking he should take her on into the cabin, but then realizing it would be as cold inside as it was outside here. At least it was blocked from the hard wind. He'd hurry and get Toy in the shed, feed him, and then return. The blizzard was so bad that he couldn't even see the horse shed. Luckily, someone in the past had put up a pole railing from the porch corner to the barn to have something to follow in a blinding blizzard.

He got the girl off the sled, into the cabin, and onto his bunk—a real struggle for a cold, stiff person to accomplish, but he did. Then he got the fires in the heater and cookstove and started the coffee.

When he checked the girl, she was still unconscious, but sort of moaning, like she was trying to come awake. He got some water and washed her dirty face. As he looked at her clean face, he was startled! She reminded him of a girl he used to know, so many years ago. She squinted her eyes, reaching out with her hand and trying to say something, like "Dan, where am I? Don't leave me, she whispered," but before he could answer, she had slumped back on her pillow sound asleep or passed out, he didn't know which. Her breathing seemed all right and her pulse strong, so he decided she was just asleep again.

He pulled his one big easy chair around beside the bed facing the heating stove and sank back into it. He'd sure like to have a swig of that coffee, but right now he was too tired to get up and go get a cup, plus, she still had ahold of his hand. Maybe a Durham would taste just as good he guessed, so he went fishing through his shirt pocket once more. Then he remembered; he couldn't roll a quirley with one hand.

Chapter Four

The night wore on as Cougan sat there thinking. His thoughts drifted back to a time something around ten years ago, when he had first drifted into the small high desert town. The first person he noticed when he crawled out of the stage, which was what they called the old car that hauled the mail out there, probably a holdover from a few years back—but anyhow the first person he saw that he could remember, resembled this girl. He had wondered how she got the scar on her leg.

The second time, she was working behind the counter in the dining room of the hotel. He was only fifteen and too bashful to be able to talk to a girl, but still, she created an interest in him on first impression. He could remember how he had stepped back to be in line with the mirror which was behind the counter, as he stepped up. He wanted to make sure that his hat was pulled down just the right amount so as to give him that personalized, distinguished look. That green silk neckerchief had to be just right too, he knew.

Cowboy Cougan

When she brought the menu to him, he could hardly read it, because she made him so nervous. She stood right there in front of him waiting for his order.

"Are you working around here?" she asked, sort of teasingly.

And all poor old Cougan could get out was "No, not yet." Even that had sounded squeaky to his ears.

"Oh, then you're planning on going to work here," she tormented him, for undoubtedly she had seen the difficulty he was having. "On one of the hay outfits?" she went on.

"No, out with the UC wagon," he answered, a little more confident.

"Oh! You're going to be a big, wild cowboy! Then she sort of snickered. That's when Cougan didn't reply. "Well, I ain't got all day. Have you made up your mind what you're gonna eat, cowboy?"

"Yeah," he answered, as he raised up from the stool and pitched the menu back down to the counter. "Nothing here."

Then he turned and stepped proudly from the dining room with the air of a young banty rooster. He wasn't sure he could get on with the UC's, due partly to his only being fifteen years old, but he'd heard that their horse wrangler had quit a few days before. They probably wouldn't ask his age because he was plenty big enough to do a full day's work.

He got on with the outfit and went out with the wagon. He didn't see the girl again until about six months later in

Chapter Four

the fall, when the wagon crew trailed a beef herd into the headquarters of the ranch. The last day had been a short trail, and they were in shortly after noon. There wasn't anything doing the rest of the day, so everybody piled in an old jalopy and went in to see how things were clicking in this great desert town, population 500, including dogs.

Some of the boys set into slopping up beer. It had been quite a while since they had been to town. Another month and they would have dried up and blowed away, they swore; but little old Cougan—they called him "Tip" in those days—was too young to get liquor in the bar so he amused himself by just sauntering around and looking the town over. The only thing he found interesting was a poster on the bulletin board in the hotel lobby.

There was to be a dance in the high school gym that night, and everybody was invited. "Tip," as he was known now, wouldn't admit to himself that he was looking around hoping to find that pretty girl. He had slicked up pretty good before coming to town, so he thought. As he sat watching the boys soak up beer, maybe he'd just take in the dance. Who knows? It might be interesting.

Tip had noticed a green and yellow plaid wool snap-buttoned shirt in the store window; so when he made up his mind to take in the dance, he went and bought the shirt. He made quite a picture, he thought that night when he had gotten ready for the dance.

He had changed shirts in the hotel washroom, where there was a fairly large mirror, big enough anyhow. If he stood back just right, he could get an overall picture of himself. "If this don't take her eye," he thought to himself, "I don't know what might."

He did reflect quite a picture as he stood there, from his new oxblood colored boots to his Levi's, which had been sent to a laundry and now had a crease staying in them enough to make them look pretty sharp. The light yellow horse hide leather jacket (no fringe) really stood out, with the collar and front of the new shirt showing. He liked the way that green silk neckerchief blended with the rest of his outfit. He decided that the finishing touch, the thing that really added class to his whole appearance, was the new "California" black hat that he was wearing.

Tip didn't notice the door behind him opening and another cowboy coming in, so when he turned to see how he looked from the side and caught a glimpse of the fellow watching him, he was embarrassed, almost unbearably, especially when he saw that it was one of his own outfit.

"Pretty damn western, kid," the puncher teased. "If you don't win one tonight, it'll be because you're too busy fighting off these "city nesters."

Tip was embarrassed more by the puncher's kidding, but secretly he was very pleased by what he said. All he could do in the way of answering was to grin sheepishly at the puncher as he strolled past him and out onto the night.

Tip talked one of the punchers into buying him a pint of liquor that evening. He didn't want that much, but he was afraid they'd laugh at him if he asked them to get him any less. "A little shot of "red-eye" sure helps a fellow to get around over those unfamiliar dance floors," Tip had said in explanation of his request for the liquor.

The puncher who bought it for Tip told him, "Be careful, Tip. Don't take on more than you can handle." He wasn't a large fellow in stature and hardly ten years older, but those

Chapter Four

ten years had been spent from Mexico City to Calgary, and he had the scars to prove it. Like Tip, he also was an orphan of the range, with no bonds to hold him anyplace; however, he sort of liked the UC's, so had worked for them several times in the past few years. It seemed as though he had taken a shine to one of these nester's girlfriends, and the nesters ganged up on him one time when he was pretty drunk and beat the H-E-double L out of him. He'd just let it pass off for a while, waiting for the time he'd catch them when there wasn't more than two of them together. He figured then he'd settle the score. The nester had told around how one of them had worked him over, when he hadn't come right back at them.

"I reckon I'm not much force, according to some of those nester cowmen," he said to Tip, but I think I'll saunter down towards the dance after a bit. Then he hesitated a minute and went on: "Be careful, Tip, these city fellers and nesters around here don't care much for UC cowboys!"

Tip and the puncher stood looking at each other for a minute, as though there was a mutual understanding coming between them.

Then the puncher continued once more. "I'd go with you now, but you know I've been around here for quite a spell, and there's liable to be some people there that won't appreciate my presence, so you just go ahead and have a little fun for a while; mebbe then I'll come down and look things over."

"Okay," was Tip's only reply as he turned and started for the dance: a UC puncher all by himself!

The dance was in pretty full swing when Cougan arrived, so he just stood in the background and looked on for a while. Presently, he decided that now would be a good time to enter while everybody was dancing. That way, he wouldn't be quite so noticeable. Seems as though he had suddenly become quite self-conscious here amongst all of these small ranchers and townspeople and rosin jaws.

Tip stood back in the shadows for quite a while watching the dancers and trying to get a glimpse of the reason he came to the dance. It wasn't but a short while until he had success. She was here and how beautiful and graceful she looked to Tip, "like a fine saddle horse in amongst a bunch of pudden foots," he told himself.

Tip watched for several dances. As soon as she finished one dance with a fellow, another one would be there to grab her. Seldom did she get a chance to sit down. A couple of times, Tip almost had enough courage drummed up to approach her and ask for a dance, but each time before he would get started, some other fellow would come along and whisk her away. Finally the music stopped and most everybody sat down.

The orchestra acted as if they were getting ready to start again, so Tip summoned his courage up once more and got his feet working in the right direction She was sitting with two other girls when Tip walked up to her, with his hat in hand. He was truly as handsome, if not more so, than any other fellow his age at the dance. He really made a striking picture as he lightly stepped up to her and bowed slightly at the hips like he'd seen them do it in the movies. Then he almost surprised himself, his voice was so calm and steady and had such a marvelous ring to it as he asked the girl. "May I have the next dance, Miss?"

She sat looking up at him for a minute.

Chapter Four

"So beautiful," he thought, "with those deep hazel eyes."

Then, recognizing him, she replied with a sneer, "I don't dance with cowboys!"

Tip wanted to blush and do lots of other things as he stood there, as embarrassed as he had ever been in his life. The sneer she was giving him was sure plain hatred.

Why? Why did she have to be so hateful towards him? He had only talked to her once her once before. He thought of lots of harsh things in an instant that he'd like to say, but instead, he only said, "Excuse me," turned, and walked slowly away.

Tip felt pretty low now as he moved out of the dance hall, thinking that he didn't care if he ever went to another dance or if he ever saw another city girl. As he walked out into the fresh air, he remembered the pint that he had ditched before entering the dance hall. He guessed he'd drown his sorrow and go back and join his outfit at the bar. He couldn't buy drinks, but at least he could be in the company of some real people.

He sat sipping on his bottle, thinking how events had turned out and thinking that he had been pretty weak to consume the bottle, just because he had been beaten the first round. He believed he'd go back into the dance. A new plan was forming in his mind. Another little sip of whiskey, and he'd made his mind up, so he cached his bottle away again. He sauntered back into the dance hall like as if he owned the place. A dance was underway as he stood looking down the room of seats along the wall. This time he wasn't looking for the pretty girl. As a matter of fact, he was looking for one of the less popular girls who might be willing to dance with him. Finally he noticed one sitting by herself. "A pretty nice-looking girl," he thought, as he approached her. "Maybe she's a stranger here also." Later he found out she was with another girl who was dancing at the time.

"Hello," he said, friendly, as he walked up to her. "May I have this dance?"

She looked up and smiled pleasantly, but then said, "No thank you. I'd rather not."

"Can I sit here and talk with you then?" he asked.

She continued to look towards him. "If you wish," she replied rather nervously.

"That's sure a good tune to dance to that they're playing," Tip suggested. "I wish you'd dance with me."

She turned partly towards him then and said, "Oh, I really don't dance very good."

Tip was almost surprised at himself when he said, "You probably dance much better than I do." Then he gently caught hold of her hand as he rose from his chair, and turning towards her, said, "Let's give it a try anyhow."

She sort of half smiled then, nervous but glad that he had been persistent. She said, "Sure," and away they swung to the slow, easy rhythm of the dance band.

The ice had been broken now. Cougan had introduced himself to the girl, and during the night she introduced him to several of the other girls, with whom he laughed and really had a fine time. Not once did he look towards the

Chapter Four

girl he had come to the dance to capture. While dancing, he had almost danced into her and her partner, but every time he would hurriedly turn so as not to let her catch him looking at her.

Several times through the dances, Tip noticed that fellows with whom the pretty girl had been dancing would bump into him. They let on like it had been accidents at first, but when he good naturedly said, "Excuse me," they sneered or laughed at him. He let things pass for quite a while, but then after a fellow of about his own size and build, but perhaps a little older, had bumped him excessively hard, Tip turned towards him and said, "I'd be careful about doing that anymore, fellow," to which the fellow only laughed with a sneer and danced away. Tip just passed the incident off after a few minutes and then went on about his dancing, having a good time.

The band leader announced that after one more dance, everybody would take a break for a while for midnight supper, so Tip sought out the first girl he had danced with, whose name was Macy, and asked her for the dance and if she would go to supper with him. She really was a nice girl, he had found out. She answered that she would be delighted, since her girlfriend's date had shown up. While they were dancing, the fellow who had bumped him so hard earlier, danced up close to Tip and said in a whisper, "If you think you're tough, meet me out in back of the dance, and I'll teach you some manners, cowboy."

Macy heard him and asked Tip, "What are you gonna do?"

"I asked you to supper," Tip replied.

They danced on for a while, then Macy said, "That fellow is quite a bully here at school. He has beat up on several of the boys, and they say he's an awfully dirty fighter." Tip had been thinking all this time how he'd like to meet the bully, but then he'd asked Macy to supper, and he didn't want to stand her up. Just then he noticed his puncher friend at the front of the hall where quite a few people were gathered getting ready to go to supper. A plan struck him.

"Macy," he asked, "will you promise me something?"

"What is it?" says she.

"That you won't say anything about what's to happen, and that you'll go with my friend, and that you'll give me a rain check on the supper date?"

A plan had also struck Macy, as she spied the cowpuncher at the doorway, who, she figured, must be Tip's friend, for she knew the puncher was also a UC man. "It's a deal," she returned as the dance ended and they moved towards the front of the hall.

After Tip introduced Macy to his friend, he asked them to go on ahead to the supper room and get in line; telling them, as he winked at his friend, that he'd be along in a couple shakes. The pal said they'd wait, but Tip insisted they go on, and when Macy said, okay, well there wasn't much else to do but go.

Tip waited until they got out of sight; then he headed out back of the dance hall. There were several young people waiting when he got back there, among them the pretty girl.

Chapter Four

"Ah, here comes our big brave cowboy," the bully boasted as Tip neared. "You better start saying your prayers, because I'm gonna pound you to where your own mother won't recognize you." With this, he made a wild rush towards Tip with his head lowered like a bull on the charge.

There wasn't much time for thinking, but the moon was shining and gave enough light for Tip to see all he needed to. He mainly squared off and braced himself as the bully came rushing in, but an instant before the contact, and as quick as lightning, Tip stepped to one side, drawing his arm back as far as possible, his left fist even with his waist, and then sending it crashing forward with the power and snap of a jack mule. There was a sickening crunch as his knuckles met the solid bone of the bully's forehead. From the bully, there came the sound like that of a bag when stuck with a knife. The motion was almost too fast to watch, but with the squeal, his body came to a halt. Then he just sort of straightened up and fell over backwards. There he lay, all sprawled out, not making a sound but that of troubled breathing.

Then a small group of young men rushed in towards Tip, shouting their intentions of getting that damned puncher.

Out of the corner of his eye, Tip noticed a lone figure advancing rapidly from the other direction. For an instant he thought they were piling in on him from all sides, but then he recognized the very welcome voice of his pal, who hollered, "Stay with 'em, kid, we can lick the whole damn bunch of 'em."

Tip was busy trading knuckles with how many fellows, he really didn't know. He was just having a good time and not the least angry until someone landed a haymaker right square on his old button.

The blood flew, and Tip saw red, but he didn't go down. Instead, he just became furiously wild and then just plain mad, but coolheaded. Now every punch he sent out had the force of a jackhammer behind it. His summer of hard work and clean living had built up his stamina to where it wouldn't wear out, and with every punch he landed now, somebody went down and stayed there. It was just in a matter of minutes or seconds; who knows which is the longest at a time like this? Anyhow, the fight was over and those who weren't sprawled out were slinking away, nursing sore heads.

Tip's thoughts were interrupted by his partner's saying, "I'm right proud of you, kid. You're gonna make a man yet."

That compliment from such a scarred up old fighter really made Tip feel good. Then he saw Macy watching. "I thought you promised you wouldn't tell," he said, scoldingly.

"She didn't," the puncher put in quickly. "She just grabbed ahold my hand and jerked me around here, saying nothing. I figured the rest out myself."

To that, Tip said he'd see if he could find some wash water. Then they'd see if there was anything left to eat. "This exercise sure makes a fellow hungry," he went on jokingly.

The rest of the night went on without further interruption. When the dance was over, Tip walked Macy home.

Chapter Four

He had been joyful all night, but when they started towards Macy's house, he became rather moody.

"What's the matter, Tip?" Macy asked. "Are you sad because you spent the night and didn't get to dance with Bobbie?" As a word of explanation, she continued. "I saw you speak to her when you first came in."

"No, that's not it, Macy," he answered frankly. I was thinking about you." Macy stopped and looked up to Tip in disbelief, but she didn't say anything. Tip went on. "You see, tomorrow or the next day, the wagon will be pulling back for the high country, and I don't know when we'll be back down in this country again. Probably not until sometime before Christmas."

"Will you come to see me then?" she asked.

"I don't know," he said bluntly, hating himself instantly. Then he went on seriously, "But Macy, there's one thing I do know. I have really enjoyed tonight, being with you."

"Then you won't forget me right away?" she said sadly.

"I reckon I could never forget you—or tonight," he said, sort of perplexed as he thought of his sore and swollen nose.

Then they were at Macy's house, and before Tip knew what had happened, Macy said, "I've had a wonderful time tonight, Tip," She brushed his cheek with a kiss and was gone inside. Tip stood in bewilderment for a minute. He had caught a glimpse of Macy's face in the moonlight when she had turned towards him. It had looked so lovely then, and he was sure there had been tears in her eyes. They looked so liquid in the moonlight, but now she was gone;

so Tip shrugged his shoulders and turned back towards where his pals would be. What now? He didn't know.

The wagon pulled back to the high range the next day, as Tip had figured it would. The days, weeks, and months slowly went by, until the last herd had been rounded up and started for winter range.

"December first!" Tip had heard somebody say this morning as he stood in front of the cook's fire, trying to soak in a little heat.

"You gonna eat, boy?" the cook asked, as Tip stood there thinking about the winter camp where they'd be staying. It wasn't but just a few miles from town.

"Now you just listen here, Sonny," one of the other punchers grinned. "Just 'cause you're in a rush to get back down in the valley, so's you can fight some more over them girls, don't mean the rest of us gotta be jumping around here in the night."

Tip only grinned good-naturedly to this, as he tore into his beefsteak, eggs, biscuits, and gravy.

It had been too busy all fall to spend much time worrying about the girls. He had been trying to learn, picking up every bit of cow and horse savvy that came his way. Now that the last homeward trip was actually underway, he found that through no effort of his own, he was continually seeing that pretty girl, Bobbie, in his thoughts. He considered about Macy too, but this seemed to be more about how to keep from hurting her feelings than anything else.

Chapter Four

On the afternoon of the fifth day of moving, he shut the gate of the winter horse pasture behind his tired, gaunt, hard-worked remuda. The long hard days of the fall roundup were over. Of course, they'd be too busy all the rest of the winter working the cows and weaning and all, but the days would be a lot shorter and easier, and they'd be sleeping in a good warm bunkhouse instead of teepees and out on the ground. "It will sure seem funny to stick my legs under a dining table again after so many months squatting on my heels and sitting cross-legged to eat," he told himself as he could see the first puffs of smoke coming from the chimney of the cowboys' cookshack. "Yeah," Tip grinned. "If those lazy hounds ain't licked 'er all up while I been out trying to get things shaped up so's we can move. Sure don't take old Cookie long to get things going.

"Come on here, Warrior," he told his old wrangle horse, as he pulled his head reluctantly away from watching the remuda spreading out as they grazed. "Let's go get some coffee."

Tip wasn't different from any other cowpuncher. He had given quite a lot of thought to the next time he would get to go to town. It would sure sound good again to hear the sounds of civilization, with its juke boxes and pretty girls. The afternoon almost passed too fast with all the work he had to do before he helped the cook clean up the cookshack and they all moved in. Damn the horse wrangling anyhow. It wasn't so bad when they were out with the wagon. The worst thing riding there was moving every few days, but here now in winter camp, the job would be too much chore-work. Sure hoped that wagon boss would do what he'd mentioned awhile back! He'd told Tip that an older fellow, too stove up to ride much anymore, had hit him up for the winter wrangling job. If Tip would like to go on as a puncher, then he might put the old man on.

Cowboy Cougan

Tip was sitting his wrangle horse, waiting that evening when the last of the cowboys loped into camp. The cook had promised he'd hold up the supper until he'd gotten through with his work, so that Tip wouldn't be left behind working when the rest of the crew headed for town. The wagon boss had mentioned that since they'd all been out for almost three months with no time off, maybe they'd all better take it easy for two or three days.

Nothing of importance had happened in the little cowtown since then. To heck with it. He figured he'd savvied enough about handling cows and cowhorses, to make a hand on a big ranch. It was time to drift.

Chapter Five

After working on several different "wagons," Tip went to "rep" for his Uncle Sammy in the army. He got that out of his mind; remembering he'd been wounded, and finally got back to the States, all hyped up and super sensitive. He thought if maybe he could get a cowboy outfit back together and find an isolated ranch for a while, he could get himself straightened out. He picked up the cowboy gear he needed, a piece at a time, finding a good bridle hanging up in a bar and a good Hamley saddle at a big farm sale. The rest of the necessary items, he found here and there. He finally drifted into Hardin, Montana, where one bright light in the business area beckoned him into the "Cowboy's Bar" for a little nip.

After a bit, a cowboy-looking feller came closer and introduced himself. "I'm a local and I've lived here in this area all my life. You don't look like a native. My name's Lambert, "Lamb" for short, 'cause I'm such a meek little sheep! I work on a large ranch upcountry from here."

"Howdy. Mine's Tip. I'm just on the drift, looking for something for a spell."

Then Lamb came out with something like, "You might just be the cowboy I'm looking for. Well, this ranch has a really good winter area in Big Basin, where cattle winter out all season long on last summer's feed. Me and another Indian have been wintering there together for the last three winters. My partner is an old-time Indian. You see, this is mostly Crow Reservation country, and I'm even half Indian myself. So, we have lots of privileges that full gringos don't have. We can hunt or fish or do most anything we want on the "rez."

"My pard is getting old, and says he don't want to spend another winter in the Basin, so I says I'll try to find a man to take your place. It's a beautiful spot, and the winters are mostly good, down there in the Basin. Of course, this far north, an occasional blizzard will show up, but we have a good log cabin and stock it with everything we might need through the winter. It's a tough place to get in and out of in the winter. There's a good big meadow down there, and we have a big old team and haying equipment, so we get enough good hay put up in the summer to feed our horses good all winter.

"With your size, we've got one horse I'm sure you'd like," he chuckled. We call him "Toy," because he's so small. He probably don't quite reach 17 hands and has to be fat to weigh over thirteen hundred pounds! He's a whale of a horse, even though he's a little cranky; but you are "mounted," if you're cowboy enough to ride him. How about coming and spending the winter up there with me?"

Chapter Five

"That's how I come to be in the Basin and riding old Toy," Tip reminisced.

He looked around, noticing it was starting to get light. The blizzard was still howling outside. That brought him up short. "Damn," he thought. "I've been sitting here all night, holding that girl's hand, and reminiscing about every event that happened since I first came to Lakewood, up until last night!"

And worrying about the way things went, he stopped in front of the heating stove. Thinking he might as well, he set the coffee pot back on the stove. A cup of it might make him feel better.

He decided to go ahead and wash the girl's face again. Maybe something would come of it.

Cold water has many different effects when it touches the skin of a sleeping person. He himself knew what it would do for a throbbing head full of alcohol fumes. Not that he thought the girl was in that condition, but he thought it might slow down some reaction taking place and make her feel better when she did awaken. He was about finished when the girl regained consciousness, looked around and saw a man holding her hand.

She was wondering what she was doing in a bed, unable to move, when she opened her eyes wide and looked up silently for a minute. A million thoughts ran through her mind. "Where am I? Who is this man? And why am I here?" Then she thought she could remember an explosion or something and sailing through the air. Again, she came out with "Dan," but she didn't know why. "Dan, I hurt all over. I'm thirsty, and I feel like I need to go potty. Can you help me?"

How could he help her? The outhouse was way out back behind the cabin. The blizzard made it impossible; it was still howling too bad to be out in it. His thoughts raced to the past, when he'd been hurt and in a hospital, almost totally unable to do anything for himself. It had been embarrassing, but the nurses had done everything for him including washing and cleaning him up afterwards.

He surmised if a woman nurse could do all that for a man, then in an emergency, a man could do that for a female, regardless whether she was old, or young and beautiful like her. It might help, letting her think he was "Dan," a former boyfriend, or perhaps a close friend of hers.

As he got a cup of water for her, his thoughts ran, "Do the best you can. You'll have to help her, but how? Maybe if you get all the pillows to pry up her shoulders, it will help; but what to do for a bedpan?" He didn't think it was feasible to try to lift her off the bunk. Besides that, he didn't have a "thunder bucket." Just an old outhouse out back! Maybe his small washpan would work. If he could get the second chap leg off and get her slacks down, then with one arm under her, he could lift her enough to get the pan under her.

He got the pan close by and commenced to remove her lower clothing, finally working her slacks down off her hips. "Damn! Her panties were a mess! The only thing now, he guessed, was to take his knife and cut the legs to get them out of the way. Embarrassing, but necessary.

He finally got the washpan under her. It helped that she kept thinking it was Dan who was helping her. When he got the pan out of the way, her words came out, "Dan, can you get me a washrag and some water?"

Chapter Five

He got it, but she couldn't do what she wanted by herself, so he helped her. Embarrassing again. She turned her head away then and lay so still for so long that he thought she had gone back to sleep again, until she blinked her eyes and looked up.

He said, "You're okay, Miss. How do you feel?" he asked softly, not certain that she was wholly awake.

"Like I been clawed by a grizzly bear," she answered feebly. "Is everybody else all right?"

"It was a pretty bad wreck, Miss," he answered evasively. "How many people were on the plane altogether?" he asked.

"There were four other passengers, besides the pilot," she said weakly.

"No relatives of yours?" he asked hesitantly.

"No," she stated. "The other passengers?" He didn't answer, not wanting to upset her, but he looked grim. "They were—? *All?*" She stopped as Tip nodded his head in the affirmative.

He sat in a daze, holding her swollen hand. Was it the girl? It had to be. Again he turned his eyes to her left hand and confirmed that she wasn't wearing a ring. He sat for long minutes thinking about the girl and telling himself that this couldn't be her. His memory was all intermingled with the night's happenings. He was thinking in circles. Nothing was clear.

"Damn," he thought. He couldn't even remember what she had looked like the last time he had seen her. It had been seven years since he had joined the army. They had needed men badly then. He hadn't even taken his furlough when he got through boot camp. Instead he had volunteered as a replacement and was shipped right out.

The blizzard howled all day. When feeding time came, he was able to work his way out to the barn to see about Toy and feed him again. When he came back in, she sort of blinked her eyes, and said something that sounded like she was hungry. Tip came to her side and asked, " Are you awake? Do you feel all right?"

Feebly, she answered, "My leg feels funny. I feel sort of beat."

Damn again! What could he feed a gal like her, in her shape? He said, "Maybe I could make you something hot if you feel you could eat some."

"A slight bit, maybe." Then again, "Where am I?"

"In a cabin, in a line camp, way up high in the mountains. I'll see about some food."

He knew there was lots of food in their sawdust-insulated pantry. He'd go see what he could find. After sorting through several shelves, he noticed a label that said, "chicken broth." That might do the trick. He opened the can and heated it up. It had a good taste to it. He'd try it on her. He spooned several bites to her lips before she seemed to get interested in it. He was able to get some down her, and she finished the broth before she fell back to sleep again. She seemed more content when he was close to her. Maybe she thought he was Dan. He stayed there in the cabin watching over her, just doing the necessary chores, until after dark.

Chapter Five

He remembered seeing an army cot in the storeroom. That would be better to sleep on by her bunk than the chair.

In the middle of the night, he was awakened by the lack of wind noise. The blizzard must have quit. Morning would tell. Sure enough, the sun came up. When he raised up, she had her eyes partly open, looking toward Tip, with a question, "Who are you? Where am I?" Then she'd lain back like she'd gone to sleep again.

Tip came to her side and asked, "Are you awake? Do you feel all right?

Feebly, she answered, "My leg hurts, and I'm so tired."

Tip offered, "I might make some hot cereal if you feel you could eat some."

"Maybe a little bit." She managed to get down some of the cereal before she fell back to sleep again.

After tidying up some, Tip went out to take care of Toy. The sun had come up quite a ways while he was in the shed. He wasn't quite through when he thought he heard men's voices. Getting outside, he saw three men mushing down through the snow. The first he recognized was Slow Elk; then the ranch boss, and a third man who looked like a Crow Indian. "Howdy," was their greeting. "We had to leave our Jeep on the rim. The drifts looked so bad down here, we figured we'd better come see how you'd made out."

"You're sure welcome here. I'm okay, but I've sure got a problem! A plane wrecked out in the Basin. I found several bodies, and one live lady. She's sorta semi-conscious; she's got a broke leg, but seems to know nothing. I think she's all right other than the broke leg."

The ranch boss asked all the questions about how and where, and if there were any other people in the plane wreck.

"Yes, all dead. I laid out their bodies beside the wreck. They'll all be covered by snow now, but they'll show up as the snow melts.

Following all the questions, the ranch boss came out with, "I guess we better see if we can get her back up to the Jeep and on to Headquarters and a doctor. How will we move her?"

"Well," Tip said, "I'll saddle my little pony, Toy; tie her back on the airplane metal sled I used to get her here, and pull her as far as I can. Maybe you three guys can help get her over the bad places, where I can't pull her with Toy."

Quizzical looks came over all three men's faces, because they all knew Toy wasn't a gentle enough horse to do something like that!

When they got her bundled up, and both legs wrapped up in his chaps and ready, Tip led Toy out of the shed, saddled. The guys couldn't believe what they saw! How still and quiet Toy acted as Tip mounted him with the rope and started the sled with her in it.

The two steep miles to the top of the rim was a struggle. The trail was drifted over too deep to use much of the way. With the three men, they were able to keep going, each helping with the sled when needed in order to get through the bad places. It only took close to three hours to get to the top.

Chapter Five

After all the talking, the ranch boss said, "Tip, you better come down to headquarters." Joe, who was a Crow Indian, said he and Slow Elk would go back and stay in the cabin. He was as tall as Tip; he could ride Toy back on Tip's saddle, as his legs were long enough to reach Tip's laced-tight stirrups.

Tip agreed to this, and everybody left; three to headquarters and two heading back down into the Basin line camp.

Chapter Six

The trip to the top with the sled was slow and rough. Then the sled had to be put crossways on the back of the Jeep for the ride to headquarters. The girl fretted a lot, but never complained. When they came into the headquarters, the ranch boss spotted Bob Small, a rancher whose wife was a nurse in the hospital before she got married.

"Will you go ask your wife if she will come help take care of this injured girl we have here, until the doctor gets here?"

The doctor soon arrived to check on the girl. She didn't have any identification on her, and she still couldn't remember her name. Tip told them he thought her name might be Bobbie, but he couldn't come up with a last name.

After getting the chaps-splint off her legs and checking her thoroughly, the doctor suggested that since they had lots of room and help, it might be best to leave her here, instead of travelling another two or three hours to a town hospital.

Chapter Six

Inquiries had already come into the ranch headquarters from some airport investigators concerning a missing plane. They wondered if anyone had seen, or knew anything about, an airplane flying over some part of that country. After hearing Tip's story, he was requested to stay at headquarters until a helicopter showed up, since he might be able to direct them to the plane crash.

The 'copter showed up the next morning. After flying up and into the Basin, finding a place to set the 'copter down, and checking all that was visible, they returned to the headquarters. They said Tip would need to stay there until they got a snowcat and trailer trucked in to go get the bodies from the plane crash, and anything else they could bring out that might help determine the cause of the crash.

Bobbie was doing better. She could sort of remember she'd been in some kind of wreck. Her friend Dan, whom she'd been murmuring about, wasn't there anymore. She wanted to know, "How did I get out of the wreck? Where is Dan? And how did I get here? And where is here? Where am I?"

They told her, "A cowboy found and rescued you and has brought you all the way here. This is the headquarters of this ranch, which includes the Basin and all this surrounding area.

She considered all that and then asked, "Where is that cowboy?"

The reply was, "He's back with a large crew to show them where to go to find the crashed plane and take care of everything that's possible, considering the weather."

Bobbie's mind, with the temporary amnesia, was starting to flicker in and out. She wondered about it all. So much of it was missing, but little bits and pieces were working their way to the top. She'd like to meet the man who saved her life.

The day Tip got back to headquarters with the rescue car, he was told that the girl he called Bobbie would like to meet the man who saved her life. The doctor just happened to be there that day to see how she was. Tip met him and asked how she was doing.

"Wonderful! I feel you did a good job with your chaps and splinting her leg, which is in a cast now."

"It was so dark that night, I couldn't see much. How did it look when you got it cleaned up?"

"Good, but it had a bad scar on it, I think it was from a previous accident of some kind. Her leg sure looks good and will be usable pretty soon, in a couple months or less."

"Thanks, doc. That's wonderful news." (Now he knew for sure it was the girl.) "Can I see her now?"

"Sure thing," the doc said.

Weak kneed, Tip entered the room. As he stepped through the door, he was spellbound. There, wrapped up on the bed, with pillows up behind her back, sat the most beautiful girl he had ever seen. Wavy, satiny, long dark hair adorned with a beautiful blue bow, hung over the front of her shoulders.

Bobbie had been wondering if, by some miracle, this was the cowboy she'd been hunting for, for so long. On

Chapter Six

seeing him, she knew. With one hand slightly waving and a smile that thrilled him through his whole body, she whispered, "Hello Tye."

"My name's Tip," he weakly got out; he was so spellbound that all he could do was stammer.

She answered, "To me, it has always been Tye, ever since the day you came into Lakewood on the stage. We never spoke to each other, but I was so impressed with you, I asked one of the stage drivers who you were. It has been 'Tye' to me ever since."

He said, "Tip Cougan and Banks, but I don't have the right to use that. The Banks name, I mean."

"How did you know my name was Bobbie Saunders?"

"I didn't know your last name until now. But everybody knew Bobbie, the prettiest girl in town! If you were so impressed with me, why did you give me such a cold shoulder in the restaurant, the first time I came in and you brought me the menu?"

"You seemed to ignore me, so I decided to teach you a lesson and treat you the same way. When you got up and walked out, I was flabbergasted to think you weren't a bit interested in me.

Tip explained, "I was too young and bashful to visit that day."

"And then there was the dance," Bobbie went on. "I thought I'd get even, telling you I didn't dance with cowboys! And then, through the dance, you ignored me and danced with Macy and the other girls. We were all friends. I was tickled when the town bully invited you out behind the school. I thought, 'He'll take the starch out of you!' But then, I was so thrilled when you whipped him so quick and easy. I never liked him and his bullying ways anyhow. And then you were gone. You went back out with the wagon and never came back to town. I asked at several different places, but could never find out anything about you."

Tip answered, "I drifted for a while, from one wagon to another, for two or three years or so. Then the Army got me."

"Don't you have some folks? I asked all over, but no "Banks" I got ahold of ever heard of you.

Tip said, "The Banks's were an older ranch couple that I got acquainted with at a horse sale one time when I was young and on the prowl."

"Didn't you have parents?"

"Not that I could ever remember. I stayed with the Banks's awhile. I think they found an old paper in my coat pocket that read as near as they could make out, 'Tip Cougan' or something like that. The called me Cougan, and I guess I took their last name of Banks as mine."

"What did you do after you left Lakewood?"

"Like I said, I drifted from one outfit to another until I joined the Army. "I came back once to Lakewood to look up Macy, but found out she'd gotten married and moved away. You'd also left by then." I looked lots of places for you, but couldn't learn anything. After the service, and being all mixed up mentally about what I wanted to do, a fellow

Chapter Six

offered me an isolated winter job. I figured it might be a good place to get ahold of myself again. That's what I was doing, out riding my horse in a snowstorm, when an airplane crashed right in front of me. And I found you!

"When I got you back to camp and washed your face, I finally got a good look at you. I was devastated! You had to be that same beautiful girl, the one who had instantly appealed to me the first time I ever saw her, when I got off the "stage" that night in Lakewood.

When I found you at the crash, you were lying a little ways away from most of the wreckage, and I had a strange feeling I knew you somehow.

"I could tell you had a broken leg. I straightened it out the best I could and wrapped my chaps around it Then I remembered the scar on a girl's leg I used to know. I had the leg already wrapped up, so my question was never answered until a few minutes ago, when the doctor said that your leg looked good, but you had a bad scar on it that looked old.

"Bobbie! The only girl I've ever been more than mildly interested in, in all my born days, and there you were. And now, here you are!"

Their eyes glowing, they reached out toward each other, until Tip had to step over and take her in his arms in a warm embrace. All he could say was, "Bobbie! Mine!"

They talked and visited about everything, until Bobbie finally came out with, "What will you do now?"

"I kept some contact with the Banks. They're getting older and don't have any kids. They'd like me to come home and maybe take over the ranch. It isn't a big outfit, but large enough and beautiful enough, that with the right person, it would sure be worthwhile. What would you think about that?"

With a wonderful smile, she said, "I'd love to go there and spend forever with you. When can we get married?"

"As soon as you can get around good, our dreams will come true. We'll take over the ranch and take care of the Banks. They're a wonderful old couple, and we'll all live happily forever!

Tip was not a religious man, but he looked over his shoulder and said, "Thanks, Pard! You sure were with me this time!

Glossary

Cowboy Terms

A'tall .... Alternate spelling of "at all" intended to approximate dialect pronunciations.

Batwings .... Long leather chaps with broad, winglike flaps.

Bogging .... A quick bobbing of a horse's head to loosen the reins enough to buck the rider off its back.

Chaps .... Leather pants or leggings without a seat, worn over regular pants to protect the legs.

Chinook .... Soft warm spring breeze.

Crockett's Law ... A reference to the rider digging their spurs in hard to gain control of the horse. Oscar Crockett, born in Pecos City, Texas in 1887 was a famous spur maker.

Cripes .... A euphemism for "Christ." Sometimes used in place of "damn it."

Dallied .... (Spanish - dar la vuelta): To turn around; to wrap the rope around the saddle horn when roping.

Glossary

Gunsel .... Gunman, a criminal or outlaw carrying a gun.

Haymaker .... A powerful blow with a fist, often intended to knock someone out.

Hondo .... The sliding loop in a lasso.

Houlihan .... Var. hoolihan; a special type of backhand throw which cowboys use, especially for catching horses, usually having a small loop.

Jimmycane .... Whirliwind, a swirling, funnel-like, desert dust cloud, a dust devil.

Lass rope .... Lasso, a cowboy's rope.

Line camp .... Simple camp on the outside boundary line of a ranch where cowboys stay to keep their cattle inside the line and the neighbor's cattle out.

Makins .... The materials for making a quirley, a roll-you-own cigarette.

Maverick .... Unbranded or unmarked cattle.

Oncet .... Dialect word for "once." Pronounced WUHNST.

No rest for .... An old saying that derives from the Bible, Isaiah: 57.
the wicked

Piggin' string .... Short rope or leather strap used to tie an animal's feet together to prevent it from standing up.

Quirley .... A roll-your-own cigarette.

Remuda .... (Spanish) exchange; group of geldings from which cowboys choose their mounts.

Glossary

Riata .... (Spanish) Var. reata: braided rawhide rope favored by cowboys in California, Nevada, and Oregon; commonly called a 'gutline,' much longer than grass ropes, being from 65 to 125 feet in length.

Ribbons .... Lines, leather straps used to drive horses.

Riggin' .... Rigging, western saddle.

Rosin jaw .... A hired hand who does the feeding, mechanical repairs, and maintenance on a ranch.

Rough strings ... 'Green' or untrained horses that will buck or fight anyone who attempts to ride them.

Studied .... Thought.

Sunfishing .... Bucking; jumping in the air and swapping ends and landing in the opposite direction.

Took my turns ... Dallied; wrapped the rope around the saddle horn two or three times to hold it secure when a cowboy is roping; right-handers go counter clockwise; left-handers the reverse.

Trackin' .... Moving a horse one or more steps out of his tracks where he stood while being saddled.

Woolies .... Chaps (pronounced shaps), made of Angora goat or sheepskin having very long hair for cold weather

About the Author

'Red Cloud,' as he is known in the cattle country, has been a working cowboy and horseman all his life. Raised on a ranch in Colorado, he quit school at sixteen and went to work breaking mules to drive for the ZX Ranch at Paisley, Oregon, until he got hired on 'with the wagon.' "All I ever wanted to be was a 'big ranch' cowboy. The first 30 years of my life, I didn't know I could make a living if I wasn't ahorseback. I liked punching cows, riding broncs, and driving fast horses. I took part in a stagecoach holdup at a rodeo, which eventually evolved into getting one of my own and breaking six-up hitches of Morgan horses to pull it. Two of the highlights were our 1976 stagecoach

About the Author

trip from St. Joseph, Missouri to Sacramento, California; and our invitation to President Carter's Inaugural Parade in 1977, representing the 17 western states. We started providing horses for the movies in 1975 with *The White Buffalo*. Been at it ever since, including *Tombstone*, *The Alamo*, and *Into The West*."

Red's first published work was the story of the Bicentennial stagecoach trip Stagecoach 76, in *The Tombstone Epitaph*. His current stories in *The Cowboy* magazine are of his life as a working cowboy.

Red lives with his wife on their horse ranch near Tucson, Arizona.

About the Illustrator

Margery Wolverton began drawing horses before she entered kindergarten and continues her love of making art to this day. After being married to Red for more than 50 years and seeing firsthand the western way of life, the illustrations are her attempts to capture some of those moments of the working cowboys.

www.ingramcontent.com/pod-product-compliance
Lightning Source LLC
LaVergne TN
LVHW011739060526
838200LV00051B/3249